POISONED APPLES

The Woods

The action's always there.
Where are the fairy tales about gym class
or the doctor's office or the back of the bus
where bad things also happen?
Pigs can buy cheap building materials
just as easily in the suburbs.
Wolves stage invasions. Girls spit out
cereal, break chairs, and curl beneath
covers like pill bugs or selfish grannies
avoiding the mess.
No need for a bunch of trees.
You can lose your way anywhere.

Christine Heppermann

POISONED APPLES

Poems for You, My Pretty

With photographs by various artists

Greenwillow Books
An Imprint of HarperCollinsPublishers

Library of Congress Cataloging-in-Publication Data

Heppermann, Christine.
Poisoned apples : poems for you, my pretty / Christine Heppermann.
pages cm
"Greenwillow Books."
Summary: "Christine Heppermann's powerful collection of poems
explores how girls are taught to think about themselves, their bodies,
their friends—as consumers, as objects, as competitors. Based on classic fairy tale
characters and fairy tale tropes, the poems range from contemporary retellings to
first-person accounts set within the original stories. From Snow White's cottage and
Rapunzel's tower to health class and the prom, these poems are a moving depiction
of young women, society, and our expectations. Poisoned Apples is a dark, clever,
witty, beautiful, and important book for teenage girls, their sisters, their mothers,
and their best friends"—Provided by publisher.
ISBN 978-0-06-228957-5 (hardback)
I. Title.
PS3608.E66A6 2014 811'.6—dc23 2013050903
14 15 16 17 18 LP/RRDH 10 9 8 7 6 5 4 3 2 1
First Edition

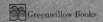

For Claudia

CONTENTS

POISONED APPLES

The Never-Ending Story ↜

Once there was a girl who wore her bones outside of her body.
Once there was a girl who thought bones looked nice.
Once there was a girl who had limbs as blue as razors.
Once there was a girl who sat by a pool in August
wrapped in a quilt.
Once there was a girl who even after she became a beast,
soft fur blanketing her cheeks, belly, and back,
still shaved her legs.
Once there was a girl who peeled grapes, who picked
at salads,
who piled leaves on top of the cheese.
Once there was a girl who dared not swallow anything
but air,
so she hid her saliva in plastic bags beneath her bed.

Once there was a girl who wrote "BLOATED WHALE"
inside the pocket of her skinny jeans.
Once there was a girl whose little sister pretended
all the dollies had feeding tubes.
Once there was a girl whose father held her tight
to stop her from doing crunches.
Once there was a girl whose mother's dreams
all became nightmares.
Once there was a girl who longed to be brave
enough to stick her finger down her throat,
to measure herself by the teaspoon,
to shrink to the size of a serving.
Once there was a girl who lay still for the doctor.
Once there was a girl whose favorite nurse called her Sugar.
Once there was a girl whose heart burrowed deep
    in the hollow of her chest
and went to sleep.

The Wicked Queen's Legacy

It used to be just the one,
but now all mirrors chatter.

In fact, every reflective surface has opinions
on the shape of my nose, the size

of my chest, the hair I wash and brush
until it's so shiny I can see myself

scribbling notes as each strand
recommends improvements.

I make sure to write them all down
when all I really want is to stop

at the market and flirt with the butcher,
ignoring his critical knives,

haggling, for once, over the cost of
some other poor creature's thighs.

Abercrombie Dressing Room ⌁

Now you believe the rumor
that they spray the clothes with perfume
every few hours because,
within these hothouse walls,
everything stinks—
the drooping skirts,
the wilted jeans,
the fading dresses losing petals,
tank tops fighting for air,
barely
hanging
on,
all so alive until
you picked them.

Sleeping Beauty's Wedding Day ↷

After the kiss and the trip to the castle comes the

showering, shaving, shampooing, conditioning,
    detangling, trimming,
moussing, blow-drying, brushing, curling, de-frizzing,
    extending, texturizing,

waxing, exfoliating, moisturizing, tanning, medicating,
    plucking, concealing, smoothing,
bronzing, lash lengthening, plumping, polishing,
    glossing, deodorizing, perfuming,

reducing, cinching, controlling, padding, accessorizing,
    visualizing, meditating,
powdering, primping, luminizing, correcting, re-curling,
    re-glossing, and spraying.

No wonder that hundred-year nap
just doesn't seem long enough.

Photoshopped Poem ✌

Some say the *Before* poem
had character.
This poem is much more attractive.
With the Healing Brush Tool
I took out most of the lines.
I left in a few
so it wouldn't look unnatural.

Prince Charming ↷

First thing through the door, Jed compliments
Mom's new haircut.

He listens to Dad go off.
"Guess we'll have to wait for baseball, Jed,
to win back Husky pride."

He brings state quarters for my sister's
lame collection. She shrieks like they are
diamonds.

Finally he guides me down
the slippery driveway to his car,
engine running, heat on high
so I won't be cold. He says, "Girl,
you look *amazing*. That sweater
makes your boobs look
way bigger."

A Brief History
of Feminism ⟿

Simon says touch your toes.

Simon says turn around.

Simon says touch your toes again.

Now wiggle a little.

Simon says he is *not* a pervert.

Simon says hop on one foot.

Simon didn't say stop hopping!

Hop closer.

Simon says hop closer.

Simon says is that a push-up bra?

Geez, honey, calm down.

Simon says calm down.
On second thought,
Simon says you're pretty cute
when you're all worked up like that.
Wanna hop your sweet self into my office
and see my sofa bed?
Simon says, we were just playing, Officer.
Simon, anything you say
can be used against you in a court of law.

Suburban Legends

Even though we don't really believe
all the crap about pale men and women,
their mouths wide as nightmares, lurching out
from the sinister trees, a trip to look for
the albino farm is as good an excuse as any
to get in that car and continue the story
of Terri, who draws on eyeliner with red pen,
and Karen deliberately spilling her vodka and Sprite
so she can take off her shirt and wave it out the car window,
and me, stuck once again with the ugliest guy,
the one with the half-assed mustache and tragic skin.
Speeding away from Westroads Mall and the PG movie
we will never see, we own this Omaha night.
Terri passes a joint with the driver.
Karen screams when the wind or cold
hands hit her bra, and I pretend nothing
is worming beneath my miniskirt,
while, not far off, a phosphorescent boy
blinks pinkly across a bonfire and says,
"Are those people for real?"

The First Anorexic ↜

Even the bruises she loves,
those bites when her mouth,
expecting resistance, sinks to the core
where the hissing begins tempting her
to scrape the flesh from every ruddy strip.

She hurries to swallow
the seeds, the stem, the clinging leaves.
Now Eve can see beyond the garden.
Now she knows there is nothing but hunger.
Each meal will be a new sweet punishment.

A SHAPE MAGAZINE
Fairy Tale ⌒

Once upon a time there was a girl who
had a good hair week! Seven cute looks
she could do at home, and their names were
Waves, Bob, Bun, Bangs, Braid, Sleek, and
Party-Ready Ponytail.

One day, while out walking in the woods
at a steady pace with short bursts of speed,
the girl met a wolf and told him, *What big
smudge-free lashes you have!*
The wolf said, *The better to see you*

*fix common makeup blunders; erase
years in minutes!* So the girl skipped
the loose powder, stuck to pastels, and
dabbed her lips with Spun Sugar
Plumping Gloss ($18), so delicious that

the wolf ate her up. The woodsman
rode by—torching three hundred calories
in just thirty minutes!—lifted his axe,
and shouted, *Adios, belly flab!*
It was a quick-and-easy workout.
The girl sprang from the wolf's
killer middle to snag fall's hottest
shoes and bags, and they all lived
happily
ever
ab-tastic.

Retelling ∽

What the miller's daughter should have said
from the start
or at any point down the line is,
no.
No, you can't drag me to the king.
No, I can't spin that room full of straw into gold.
No, not that room, either.
Or that one.
Quit asking.

No, I won't give you my necklace.
No, I won't give you my ring.
No, I can't give you the child;
the child will never exist.
End of story.

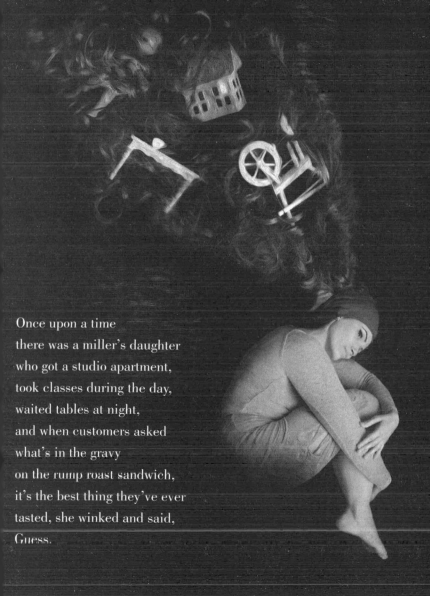

Once upon a time
there was a miller's daughter
who got a studio apartment,
took classes during the day,
waited tables at night,
and when customers asked
what's in the gravy
on the rump roast sandwich,
it's the best thing they've ever
tasted, she winked and said,
Guess.

BFF

Jill doesn't want me to feel bad.
Jill says Dylan isn't good enough for me.
Jill would let me borrow her green skirt,
but it's new, and I might stretch it out.
Jill is glad *her* parents don't force her
to buy hot lunch.
Jill knows a superchic way to do my hair
so it will hide my ginormous forehead.
Jill can teach me how to do my mascara
so my eyes look less squinty.
Jill can't help it if Dylan asked her to the movie.
Jill won't tell anyone
besides Dylan
about that time I peed my pants at Target.
Jill wishes I had made cheerleading, too,
but aren't her pom-poms cute?
Jill is *soooooo* glad we're BFFs because,
Like, who else could put up with you?
LOL!

Blow Your House In

She used to be a house of bricks,
point guard on the JV team, walling out
defenders who could only huff and puff
and watch the layups roll in.

She traded for a house of sticks,
kindling in Converse high-tops and a red Adidas tent.
At lunch she swirled a teeny spoon in yogurt
that never touched her lips and said
she'd decided to quit chasing a stupid ball.

Now she's building herself out of straw
as light as the needle swimming in her bathroom scale.
The smaller the number, the closer to gold,
the tighter her face, afire with the zeal of a wolf
who has one house left to destroy.

———

"Mannequins Make Me Feel Like a Failure."

—Claudia, age 13 ❧

So how do you think you make *us* feel?
Winter white shifts to spring floral to the bleak chill
of swimwear, and all the while we stand rigid
as you stride through the doors,
scanning the racks for answers, a little grace
that doesn't pinch.

You say you want to be created in our image.
Sorry, it's the other way around.
We look hard, but underneath we are
a mess. And if we did have the power to
flex our hands, don't you think we would
shake you like sick-and-tired mothers?

You should know how lucky you are
to have someone ask *you* the questions:
Can I help you find anything?
Can I help you?
Can I help?

If Tampons
Were for Guys 〜

Of course there are no pink wrappers,
only camo.
Forget Gentle Glide and pictures of pearls—
the box reads Smooth Ride across
the hood of a bitchin' red Porsche.

For pads with Wings, Kotex shows jet fighters.
For Heavy Flow, ninjas surf a tsunami.
For Scented, smiling blondes in bikinis
enjoy sniffing a crotch.

Panty Shields are now just Shields
or maybe Boxer Armor.
On the commercial, tanks roll through the bathroom,
manned by scowling marines in white pants.

Then it's back to *Monday Night Football*,
where both starting quarterbacks are on the DL.
"Dysmenorrhea," mutter the trainers.
In other words, cramps.

The Giant's Daughter
at Spring Formal ↩

It's bad enough
that the other girls shopped at Teeny Town,
and I'm decked out in
Tarp City,

but even through the perfume
of my pumpkin-size corsage,
Papa will smell Jack on me when I get home,
those greedy little hands.

He'll stagger around the castle
hunting for bones to grind
until I tuck him in. Then I'll toss
the bottles down through the clouds
where Mama won't find them,
and wait out by the beanstalk.

Someday I'll meet a guy
I can look up to.
One who's not a drunken oaf
or a shrimp whose jeering buddies
dared him to make the climb.

The Anorexic Eats a Salad ꙮ

Mountains rise, fall, rise again.
Stars complete their slow trck into oblivion.
A snail tours the length of China's Great Wall
twice.
All those pesky cancers—cured.
Somewhere in Lower Manhattan,
a barista finally
smiles.
Roundworms evolve into ovals.
Flatworms get chesty.
Molasses, a tortoise, and sedimentation
run the fifty-yard dash.
Results pending.
Temps plunge in hell. The devil
waxes his skis.
She has almost made it through
her first bite.

A Witch's Disenchantment ᔐ

Love charms never were my thing.
Such spells call for ingredients
missing from my cupboard.

Instead of eye of newt,
plump lips.
Instead of tongue of toad,
smooth skin.
Instead of finely ground unicorn horn
from the emerald decanter,
big tits.

My only no-fail potion:
boredom mixed with
lack of options.

A lonely traveler
winds his unmagical arm
around my waist as I stare
into the cauldron, afraid
to look up and confront
my pitiful power.

"Sweet Nothings"

Says the tag, as if my breasts are
packets of no-cal sugar substitute.

I guess "Sour Nothings" would be
a hard sell. Ditto for "The Opposite of
Something" or "Sunken Chest."
(Unless they really worked the pirate theme.)

Still, what a name for a training bra.
And anyway—training bra?
Are my boobs in obedience class?
Does this mean they'll stop playing dead?

How stupid that all I have to do
is grow two squishy lumps and suddenly
I'm man's best friend.

Weight Watchers ⌃⌐

If only I'd stopped at the front door.
If only I'd resisted the windows,
the shingles, the eaves, the gutters,
the cornices, drainpipes, and siding.

Now my poor brother Hansel is locked away
when it should be me in there,
the bony crone prodding and poking
and measuring my every mouthful.

Yet sometimes there are advantages
to having no self-control. Just yesterday,
for instance, I licked a bit of Hansel's cage,
and it tasted like peppermint fudge.

You know how I am about fudge bars—
I can never eat just one.

To My Sheep,
Wherever You Are ↶

I followed advice. Left you alone. Stopped
scanning tree trunks for snagged fleece
till I was so tired I napped under a haystack,
only to open my eyes to that empty,
overgrown meadow. Again.

But I'm happy now. I have a new job
at the library, where all the books are arranged
so they're easy to find. Even then there are no
guarantees, which is why I steal my favorites
and stack them beside my bed. I keep them

safe from the man who likes to read
in the tub, the toddler with the Sharpie marker,
the woman who stands at the circulation desk
telling me she's looked everywhere. Really,
she doesn't know what happened, it's just
gone.

First Semester Haiku ↫

Science Project

We smoked Earl Grey tea
to see if it would get us
high. Results unclear.

Virgin Math

How many inches
does it have to go in? Like,
does just the tip count?

Art History Lesson

Rubenesque: the word
for masterpiece curves. Screw you,
unsalted rice cakes.

World Lit.

Jane Eyre fan fiction.
Under her demure wool dress
"Mad Woman" tattoo.

Vindictive Punctuation ✌

Use a **period** at the end of a declarative sentence.
EXAMPLE: You have five new pimples.

Also use a **period** at the end of an imperative sentence
that does not express strong emotion.
EXAMPLE: Get some concealer.

Use a **question mark** after an interrogative sentence.
EXAMPLE: Do you really think that concealer is fooling anyone?

Use an **exclamation mark** after a sentence
that expresses strong emotion.
EXAMPLE: Sheila looks great today!

Use a **comma** to separate words
and phrases in a series.
EXAMPLE: Sheila has black hair, blue eyes, and
unbelievable skin.

Use a **semicolon** when a conjunction is omitted; it indicates
a greater degree of separation than a comma.
EXAMPLE: Sheila went to the homecoming dance with Jeff;
    you stayed home
and tried a medicated face mask.

Use a **colon** to start a list or to formally introduce
a statement.
EXAMPLE: You bought three things at the drugstore: acne wash,
    benzoyl peroxide cream,
and a one-pound bag of Cool Ranch Doritos.

Use double **quotation marks** around a direct quotation.
EXAMPLE: The dermatologist said, "Picking causes scarring."

Use an **apostrophe** to show possession, as in *Sheila's boyfriend*,
or in a contraction, as in *You're* (for *you are*) *alone*.

The Elves
and the Anorexic ～

For my party I set out brownies
and a double batch of peach cobbler.
My friends tumble in,
talking, laughing, grabbing for spoons.
Off to the side I sip Pepsi Zero
and watch, like the shoemaker
in the story, as they do the work
better than I ever could.

Runaway

In the city I can pierce my lip, shave
my head, never again have to hear,
"Hey, Blondie!"

My parents can pretend they know where
I've gone. They can tell their snooty friends
I'm away at art school and will someday

be famous for what I make, not for what I
stole and broke, for everyone I disappointed.
All these weeks being grounded, I have

figured it out. If even the best porridge
makes me fart, if the coziest chair holds a
wicked splinter, and nightmares still find me

on that just-right mattress, then why not
go for just wrong? A street corner, a blanket,
a cardboard sign, and maybe a mutt I'll call

Baby Bear because he'll be the only one
who really gives a fuck if I'm there.

You Go, Girl! ↜

You go if you have
flab, chub, pudge, blubber, jiggle, cellulite,
surfeit, suet, droop, bat wings, mood swings,
muffin top, jelly-belly, bubble butt, cottage cheese,
cankles, extra pounds, extra inches, extra chins,
wetness, dryness, tightness, looseness,
redness, yellowing, blackheads, whiteheads, the blues,
bags, blotches, dark circles, dark roots,
caking, smudging, clumping, flaking, breakage,
leakage, puffiness, creases, stretch marks, rough
patches, carbuncles, stigmas, cowlicks, split ends,
frizz, seborrhea, dinginess, drabness, dullness, shine,
tiny lines, tan lines, frown lines, smile lines, panty lines,
odor, inflammation, discoloration, or dimples
on the wrong cheeks.

But buy this cream—
only $39.95!—
and we might let you come back.

Thumbelina's Get-Tiny Cleanse—Tested ⟳

Often mistaken for Tinker Bell, this sun-loving
Nordic pixie is actually the diminutive creator of
the hottest diet craze since Papa Bear's Porridge
Control. But does her get-tough plan work?
Fairy Tale Fitness enlisted the help of a celebrity
volunteer to find out.

Miss Muffet: "After two hundred years on my tuffet,
spooning in dairy, I really should change my name
to Miss Muffin Top," the bonneted star confessed.
She'd tried switching to fat-free whey but knew she
needed a more drastic change to reach her goal
weight.

Sample Menu for Miss Muffet:

Breakfast
1 Acorn cap diced pine needle
2 Drops dew, mountain or meadow

Snack
½ Rose petal, steamed

Lunch
1 Broiled ant feeler, exoskeleton removed
⅓ Acorn cap bark chips
Mist—all you can drink!

Snack
More mist

Dinner
Pond water soup
Another pine needle
½ Acorn cap whipped dandelion fluff
Again with the mist

Results: It worked! When our editors showed up at the tuffet four weeks later, the Divine Miss M was so tiny they couldn't even *find* her! They did interview a spider that was in the area, wrapping something in its web.

Next issue: The Secret of a Svelte Arachnid—*Small portions of lean protein.*

The Little Mermaid ↶

Even before I found the globe in his study
and realized that this endless land
is really just a few stray crusts drifting
through the blue, my world had shrunk

to the size of my tender new feet
on the dance floor, each minuet
like a harpooning,

to the size of the satin pillow he lets me
sleep on beside his bed,

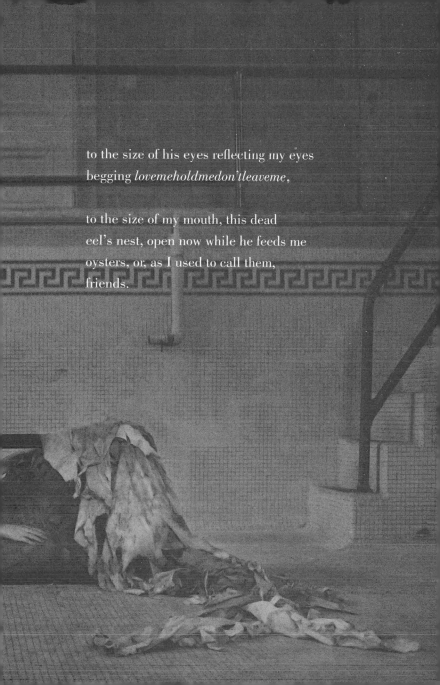

to the size of his eyes reflecting my eyes
begging *lovemeholdmedon'tleaveme*,

to the size of my mouth, this dead
eel's nest, open now while he feeds me
oysters, or, as I used to call them,
friends.

Health Class ↜

Mrs. Greco normally taught Physical Education,
which we weren't allowed to call Gym—"Jim is
somebody's uncle."

And, "Please keep your periods in Language Arts, ladies.
In this class we will discuss your *menstrual cycles*."

And, "Unless you all suddenly sprout feathers,
we will say *ova*, not *eggs*."

After the video about fertilization,
Rachel Zindler asks if what her cousin said
is true, that some super sperm
can swim right through condoms.
Mrs. Greco says, "I'm sorry, Rachel,
the school board does not allow us to cover
prophylactics."

Then Courtney Clark asks
how to tell if she is in love.
"At your age, ladies, the proper term
is *infatuation*."

We lean forward and wait
for her to explain the difference.

She tells us
to take out our textbooks
and read silently for the rest of the
period.

Ugly Stepsister

Often since the ball, when the house is draped
in sleep, I put on my robe and slippers, shuffle
past the wardrobe crammed with slack gowns,
past the door to the empty attic,
down to the kitchen, where the mice linger
just long enough to decide I am still not the one

they love. No one cares if I finish off the whole leg
of lamb, the last of the pumpkin pie.
And if I sit there dreaming until morning,
the new girl Mama hired will come in
to ask if I want tea, her soot-stained face
a perfect mask of concern.

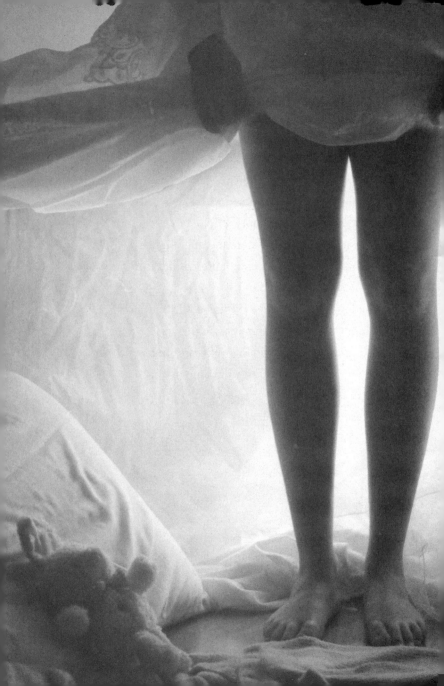

Transformation ❧

In my fantasy he is never a prince, vanilla pale
and trim, but a swarthy frog, all bulging muscle,
asking nothing more
than to eat from my plate
and sleep pooled together on my bed,
where now, alone, I ripple the sheets,
slide my fingers down
into the cool water and imagine
him there, retrieving my golden ball
again and again and again.

Boy Toy Villanelle 〜つ

G.I. Joe comes with a sword and Kung Fu Grip.
When Spider-Man shoots his webs, villains, beware!
Pony Princess Cadance has a brush, a pretty mane to style and flip.

No saddle? No bridle? For $16.99? What a gyp.
"Today's my wedding day!" squeals Cadance. Spidey, beware!
G.I. Joe comes with a sword and Kung Fu Grip;

he loves to hold a brush, style his friends' beards with fancy clips.
In his hooded spandex tux (sold separately), the groom looks so
    debonair.
Pony Princess Cadance has a brush, a pretty mane to style and flip,

and if she could pretty-please borrow Joe's sword, she could rip
down all those ugly webs in hubby's den, give the space some
    sparkle flair.
G.I. Joe comes with a sword and Kung Fu Grip,

which he pawns to open his salon—Action Hero Curl 'N' Clip.
Dreaming of villains, Spidey wakes up web-tied to his chair!
Pony Princess Cadance has a brush, a pretty mane to style
    and flip

and a Spider-Cycle she rides away at a fast clip.
Pony Princess Cadance comes with a sword and Kung Fu Grip.
G.I. Joe has a brush, pretty manes to style and flip.

Rapunzel

How foolish I was to believe that
crooning my name from below meant something
more than pressing an elevator button.

They all want to feel themselves rising
higher. They all want the girl in the tower
to pour herself into their hands.

Who's to say that, given a chance
at lower altitude, I would be different
from the rest?

Today will be the day I refuse
to lift my head from this damp pillow,
far away from the comb and the brush and the pleading
bodies always luring me down.

Light as a Feather,
Stiff as a Board ⌁

There was already enough dark magic
at those slumber parties. Still we played
the game: *You are riding the bus*
or *You are crossing the street*
or *You are walking through the park,*
and then
the brakes failed,
the lightning struck,
Your killer drags you down into the leaves. . . .

My friends chanted and slipped
a few fingers under my corpse.
If the spell worked, my soul was gone;

I was light as a feather, stiff as a board,
drifting high above their heads.

If not, they laughed and dropped me.

Nature Lesson

The dress code says
we must cover ourselves
in
ample pants,
skirts that reach well below
our lascivious knees,
polos buttoned over
the rim of the canyon,
a glimpse of which can send a boy
plunging to such depths
he may never climb back up
to algebra.

We say
that if a hiker strays
off the path, trips, and
winds up crippled,
is it really
the canyon's fault?

Red-Handed

At the Once Upon a Time Shop,
they make me check my basket,
but who cares. I have plenty of room
under my cape, a six-pack wedged against
the elastic of my gingham bikini briefs.

I buy a Get Well card for Granny,
smiling sweetly at the clerk who thinks
he's being cute when he hands me
the bag and says, "All the better to
receipt you with, my dear!"

Wolfie's waiting at our usual spot
with cigarettes. I pull out the goodies,
and the drunker we get, the more I want to
dig my nails into his pelt like
I'm going to scratch his belly, but not stop
there.

"Why, Wolfie, what a big . . ."

If that woodsman shows up now,
I will totally kick his ass.

Finders, Keepers ↶

It's not a glove left on the subway,
keys gone AWOL under the couch.
No billboard clamors, *Has anyone seen*
this missing virginity?

There has to be a better way
to say it.

Finding your sexuality?

Not so much.

Becoming a woman?

Next!

Keeping
your sense of humor?
Your dignity?
Your legs from shaking,
your teeth from chattering,
your bracelet from snagging in his hair?

Keeping your head
on his chest afterward and knowing
that crazy drum solo is playing
just for you.

Yeah.
That was definitely my favorite part.

Gingerbread ✄

I knew I had to get out of there
before the icing cracked and they discovered
that I'm burnt around the edges,
doughy in the center,
that what they thought was sugar
is salt.

If I was a good girl,
if I could satisfy their cravings,
if every dream in my misshapen head
didn't bite, I might have stayed at the table.

Wouldn't you run, too,
from such voracious love?

What She Heard the Waitress Say

Hi, my name is Stacy! Our soup of the day is souper yummy, ha-ha! It's beercheesebeanbroccolibacon.
We have two specials tonight   the crab cakes
with hollandaise, which are, like, *amazing*, and the buttermilk chicken-fried steak, which is the best thing Chef Brandon
has ever made. I could eat it for every meal, but that's me,
I'm naturally skinny and cute and not grossing out everyone
in the dining room! Should I see if Dwayne from the stockroom
will be around later to lift you out of that booth with a forklift?
I'll give you a minute to decide!

Going Under

No lifeguard on duty, and she is not at all safe
on her towel, watching the other girls bodysurf.
Her friends have no clue about the tentacles churning
close to the surface, eager to pull her under
if she so much as dips in a toe.

Okay,
one
toe.

All of a sudden she's up to her ankles
in wrappers, up to her shins, her waist, her thin
bikini strings, up to no good as the tide turns
away, disgusted, and wave after greasy wave
crashes past her salt-blistered lips.

Life Among the Swans ❧

True, no one teases me now. My new friends
and I, we don't talk much at all, really.
It's hard to make conversation
while we're gliding back and forth across
the mirror, bowing to our majesty.

For a thrill I like to shut my eyes and pretend
I never left the reeds where I waited
out that ugly winter, survived the plain
brown autumn watching the hunter's hounds
charge past me on their way to prettier game.

Big Bad Spa Treatment ∽

You are the most important ingredient in this
scrumptious day of pampering!
First our expert staff will tenderize those tired muscles
with our patented deep-tissue Massage Mallets,
leaving you loose and
gristle-free. Next, you'll soak for at least two, preferably
four to eight, hours
in a tub filled with our world-famous Aromatic Marinade
& Moisturizer
made from the finest extra-virgin olive oil, lemon juice,
garlic, and just a hint of
cayenne to give you that all-over spicy glow. Could
your Big Bad day be any yummier?
You bet! Whether your complexion is dry, oily,
or combination, our honey
barbecue facial mask will leave skin youthful, pink,
succulent, delectable, and omigod . . .

Sorry. As we were saying, we apply the mask
        while you soak, and the best part
is, there's no need to rinse it off! It absorbs directly
        into your pores to seal in
the juices. From the tub, it's mere steps back to
        our Ergonomic Butcher's Block
Massage Table for a sea salt and black pepper rub,
        though we might throw in
a few bay leaves if we're in the mood, and you know
        we are. After that, all you have left
to do is lie back and relax in our sauna, always set
        at a therapeutically optimal
400 degrees. Close your eyes. Feel the heat deep
        in your bones. We'll come and get you
when you are done.

Human Centipede Two

for Alexia ↜

is even grosser than
Human Centipede One,
my friend tells me
frequently
during third-period lunch
as I lift the bun to blot suspicious fluid
from Wednesday's burger
or Thursday's Sloppy Joe.

In the first movie the villain is a surgeon.
In the second he's just a guy with
a staple gun,
dirty knives to sever tendons,
and laxatives.

My friend lines up twelve chubby
Goldfish crackers tail-to-head to represent
the victims.

Did I know that most of the sound effects
were made with cuts of raw meat?
That at the premiere they put barf bags
on all the seats and stationed an ambulance
outside the theater for a joke, but then
a woman ended up needing it?

It's a mark of good horror,
my friend read online,
when it turns your own body against you.

Spotless

Every edge and surface
in my darlings' cozy cottage
must be better than perfect.

So I whet one razor
after another against the stony
flesh of my leg until in barely
any time at all I have seven sharp

lines

as deep as the silence of my days,
as straight as the path I ran from
the huntsman,
as red as those three drops
for which my mother named me,
or so the story goes.

They say she pricked her finger
patching a hole in my father's robe.
Dangling her hand from the window,
she thought her own blood on the snow
was the prettiest thing she'd ever seen.

The Beast ✢

Shut behind these walls only the two of us
can see the loathsome creature I am now—
in truth, have always been.

Every night the sumptuous spread,
me at the head of the table, when I really
belong on the floor, begging for scraps.

Every night the harpsichord sings
the same cruel song about love
breaking the spell,

the skimpy rose sheds another petal,
and my kind companion gazes at me
as if I am not a monster in silk and lace.

Every night the same question,
the same answer, the same stumbling
from the room while he howls

the lie that has always been my name.

Bird Girl ↩

I might as well have wings.
My hands were never good for much.
Whether braiding rugs or bread or my own hair,
my work was lopsided.
The dust in the corners felt safe
watching me wield the broom.

Fumbling. Careless. Such taunts
do not apply to the creature I am now,
one without palms and knuckles
punished by scalding wash water.

In this cage, in this feathered skin,
I am born anew.
I stretch toward the golden bars
and sing.

Assassin ✍

Once the Red Delicious clears Snow White's
epiglottis, the wicked queen moves on
to make sure a dozen dancing princesses
do-si-do no more,
to help Sleeping Beauty
find eternal rest,
to plant the foot that fits the slipper
six feet under.

Afternoons are endless meetings with the huntsman
to follow up on rumors: yes,
Gretel is becoming quite a looker,
Bo Peep has lost her baby fat,
Goldilocks has better extensions,
the third little pig was just voted
Cosmo's Sexiest Ham.

Back home in front of *The Late, Late Show*,
mixing poisons for tomorrow, she wonders
how long she can maintain this pace.
Is the Fairest's work never done?

View from the Balcony ⌇

When my sleeve slips past
the black-and-blue patchwork of skin
during my practiced royal wave,
the crowd cheers even louder,
for here's the proof!
I am the kingdom's mottled sweetheart
who can feel a single pea like a fist
thrust through the mountain of eiderdown.

The prince hammers a kiss onto my cheek.
I look down into the shadows of the courtyard
and try to spot all the others, so many
real princesses
standing stiffly on the merciless cobblestones.

Pink Champagne

That night the Platte River prowled outside our tent,
my friends and I flopped inside, a nest of babies,
not quite furless and blind, but barely

fifteen years old. We kept the music low enough
not to raise parental hackles, loud enough to drown
out the pop of the cork and then the shrieks as bubbles

swelled over the banks of the bottle, foamed down
our Dixie Cups the way rapids lathered the rocks
we later floated toward on our backs.
For once we were naked not for the sake of some
guys, but to feel the current swirling between our legs,
lifting up all those parts we had never shown

to the sun and which now glowed brighter
than every awestruck star
and one hell of an envious moon.

AUTHOR'S NOTE

If you find the dividing line between fairy tales and reality, let me know. In my mind, the two run together, even though the intersections aren't always obvious. The girl sitting quietly in class or waiting for the bus or roaming the mall doesn't want anyone to know, or doesn't know how to tell anyone, that she is locked in a tower. Maybe she's a prisoner of a story she's heard all her life—that fairest means best, or that bruises prove she is worthy of love.

But here's a great thing about stories: they can be retold.

Traditionally, fairy tales appear on the page with male names attached. The Brothers Grimm or Charles Perrault get credit for writing them down. Yet as scholars have shown, the original tellers were, in all likelihood, women. And those women were sneaky.

They understood that including fantastical elements in their tales—golden eggs, singing harps, talking frogs—worked to mask a deeper purpose. According to folklorist Marina Warner, it made the stories look on the surface like "a mere bubble of nonsense" within which it was possible to "utter harsh truths, to say what you dare" about the state of women's lives. Because they were *just* stories, right? Harmless little fantasies?

I have never been particularly brave. But when I put on the mask of fairy tales and started writing these poems, I felt powerful. I felt free to poke around inside stories that scared me or saddened me or made me mad. The more I explored the darkness, the more I realized that the forest only looks impenetrable.

My advice? Retell your own stories. Keep pushing your way through the trees, and I promise that, eventually, you will come to a clearing. And then you can dance.

—Christine Heppermann, New York

∼ACKNOWLEDGMENTS∼

I always read the acknowledgments in books, don't you? Mostly I do it for the name-dropping—she thanked the Pope! she's friends with the Pope!—and to see who all is important to the author and why. Sometimes the "why" stays a mystery. Obviously the brilliant editor, thanked first, and the darling husband, thanked last, are important, but what about all the unidentified folks in the middle?

As in the announcement of Miss America finalists, I will list my Important People in random order. I will not tell you their scores, but I assure you that they are all beautiful, talented, and smart, and each deserves a crown: Laura Ruby, Miriam Busch, Anne Ursu, Becky Stanborough, Betsy Thomas, Maura Penders, Ron Koertge, Jane Resh Thomas, Megan Atwood, Jamie Kallio, all the students and faculty in the Hamline MFAC program, Fran Hawener Cook, George Cook, Dacey Arashiba, darling husband Eric Hinsdale, Claudia Hinsdale, Audrey Hinsdale, the Dalai Lama (Can you do lunch next week? Text me.), Donna Heppermann, Don Heppermann, Ann Heppermann, Mark Heppermann, Nancy Felker, Jason Cady, Liz Heppermann, aunts/uncles/cousins/nieces/nephews/in-laws (you know who you are), the incredibly talented group of photographers whose work appears in this collection, brilliant editor Martha Mihalick, brilliant agent Tina Wexler, everyone at Greenwillow, Harvey, Raja, and Jinkx.

List of Photographs

Index of First Lines